Thy Friend, Obadiah

ALSO BY BRINTON TURKLE

Obadiah the Bold

Rachel and Obadiah

THY FRIEND,

BEAUTIFUL FEET BOOKS   CALIFORNIA

OBADIAH

WRITTEN AND ILLUSTRATED BY

Brinton Turkle

BEAUTIFUL FEET BOOKS

Copyright © 1969 Brinton Turkle

First published in 1969 by The Viking Press, Inc.

All rights reserved. No part of this book may be reproduced
in any form without the written permission of both the
copyright owner and Beautiful Feet Books, Inc.

ISBN 978-1-893103-70-2 (Hardbound)

ISBN 978-1-893103-69-6 (Trade paperback)

Library of Congress Control Number: 2018930764

Printed in the United States of America

Published by Beautiful Feet Books, Inc.
San Luis Obispo, California

for my mother and father

Wherever Obadiah went, a sea gull was following him. It followed him all the way to the candle maker's, and it was waiting for him when he came out of the shop.

When he was sent to the wharf for a fresh codfish, it hopped along behind him.

And at night when he went to bed, he could see it from his window. There it was, perched on the chimney of the shed, facing into the wind. Of all the sea gulls on Nantucket Island, why did this one go everywhere Obadiah went?

On First Day, everyone dressed up warmly and went to Meeting. The Starbuck family formed a little parade. First, Father and Mother. Then Moses and Asa and Rebecca and Obadiah and Rachel. Behind them came the sea gull, hopping along as if it were going to Meeting too.

"Go away!" said Obadiah. The bird fluttered off, but it soon came back.

"Thee has a friend, Obadiah," said Father as he turned in at the Meeting House gate.

"Obadiah has a friend!" said Moses.

"Obadiah has a friend!" said Rebecca.

"Ask thy friend to come into Meeting," said Asa.

Rachel didn't tease. She tried to take Obadiah's hand; but he didn't want to hold anybody's hand. He picked up a pebble and threw it at the bird. He missed. The sea gull flew out of sight, but when Meeting was over, there it was—waiting for him.

It got so that Obadiah didn't want to go out of his house.

At breakfast, Father said, "Obadiah, how is thy friend?"

"What friend?" asked Obadiah, his mouth full of muffin and plum jam.

"Thy very own sea gull!" said Asa.

Rebecca giggled.

"That bird is *not* my friend!" Obadiah shouted.

Mother raised a finger. "Don't distress thyself, Obadiah," she said. "I think it is very nice that one of God's creatures favors thee."

"Well, *I* don't like it," said Obadiah. "Sea gulls don't follow anyone else around!"

Soon after breakfast it began to snow. In the afternoon, Mother wrapped a woolen scarf around Obadiah and sent him to Jacob Slade's mill with some money and a sack for flour.

The bird was nowhere to be seen. "Maybe it doesn't like the snow," Obadiah told himself. "Maybe it flew away to the mainland." He was so glad it wasn't hopping along after him that he made duck tracks all the way up Jacob Slade's hill.

The miller filled the flour sack, and Obadiah gave him the money Mother had tucked in his mitten.

"Keep this, lad," Jacob Slade said, giving him a penny. "And don't let it burn a hole in thy pocket."

On the way home, Obadiah tried to slide on a patch of ice, but he skidded and fell head over heels. His hat went flying. Snow got in his ears and in his boots. His breeches got wet and so did the sack of flour. His knee hurt and the penny was gone forever in the snowbank. He was all alone on the hill. Shivering and sniffling, he picked himself up and limped home.

Sea gulls were perched on almost every housetop on Orange Street; but he couldn't find the special sea gull that had been following him. The birds were faced into the raw east wind and paid no attention to him at all.

Mother was very cross about the wet flour. She gave Obadiah a hot bath and dry clothes and right after supper she made him drink something hot that tasted awful. "Is thy knee still hurting thee?" she asked.

"It's better." Obadiah wished he felt better about the lost penny.

"Then get into bed."

Obadiah said his prayers, and as soon as Mother was gone he got out of bed and tiptoed to the window. The sea gull was not there. He got back into bed again and wondered what had happened.

The next day and the next day and the day after that, no bird followed Obadiah when he left his house. Every night he looked out of his window, but the sea gull didn't come back.

Then he saw it down at the wharf. It was with some other gulls where a little fishing boat was docked; but something was wrong. A large rusty fishhook dangled from its beak.

"That's what happens when thee steals from a fishing line. Serves thee right," Obadiah said and walked away.

He was on the cobblestone street by the blacksmith's shop when he discovered that the sea gull was hopping along behind him.

Obadiah stopped. The bird stopped. The fishhook bobbed in the wind.

"If thee is quiet, I'll try to get that off thy beak."

The sea gull didn't move.

"I won't hurt thee," Obadiah said.

The bird allowed him to come nearer and nearer. In a moment, the fishhook was in Obadiah's hand . . .

. . . and the sea gull was wheeling into the sky making little mewing sounds. It flew out toward the lighthouse. Obadiah watched until he couldn't see it any longer; then he threw the rusty hook away and went home.

As soon as he opened the front door, Obadiah smelled bread baking. In the kitchen, Mother and Rachel were just taking it out of the oven. Mother cut him a slice of the fresh, warm bread and spread it with butter. He sat on a stool to eat it and between mouthfuls he told them what had happened.

"Well," said Rachel, "thee won't see that silly old bird again."

"No," said Obadiah. "I expect I won't."

At bedtime, after she had tucked him in, Mother went to the window. "Obadiah," she said. "Look here."

He tumbled out of bed.

"Isn't that thy sea gull?"

There it was on the chimney, facing into the wind in the clear blue night!

"That's him!" said Obadiah. "He looks cold out there, Mother."

"His feathers keep him warm. But thee doesn't have feathers, Obadiah. Get back into bed quickly before thee takes a chill."

Obadiah jumped into bed again and Mother kissed him good night.

The wind whistled around the corner of the house and Obadiah snuggled down into the quilts.

"Mother. . . ."

"Yes, Obadiah."

"That sea gull *is* my friend."

"I'm glad, Obadiah. Good night."

"And Mother. . . ."

Mother turned at the door. Her candle flickered and almost went out. "Yes, Obadiah," she said.

"Since I helped him, I'm *his* friend, too."

BRINTON TURKLE

Brinton Turkle set his series of Obadiah books on Nantucket—off the Massachusetts coast—in 1805. At the time, the island was home to a large Quaker community. Turkle too was a member of the Religious Society of Friends.

Turkle was born in Ohio in 1915. He worked most of his life in New Mexico and New York City, writing children's books and illustrating 82 of them before his death in 2003. *Thy Friend, Obadiah* was awarded the prestigious Caldecott Honor in 1970. The Obadiah books reflect the beauty and simplicity of his Quaker beliefs, which he expressed this way:

> In writing, I use all sorts of tricks to capture the attention of my young audience: suspense, humor and even charm, when I can muster it. But no matter how successfully I may entertain, I am really up to something else: subversion. My abilities are implacably lined up against the hypocrisy, materialism, and brutality that so pervade our society. As my readers leave childhood behind, I hope that they will carry with them an appreciation for such alternatives as integrity, mutual respect, kindness, and reverence for life. These alternatives are in my books, and I pray that exposure to them will play a part in the construction of a better tomorrow.

Beautiful Feet Books, in cooperation with The Eric Carle Museum of Picture Book Art and Brinton Turkle's grown children—Matilda Rubin, and Haynes and Jonathan Turkle—are delighted to present these new editions of the Obadiah books for the next generation of readers. Working with Mr. Turkle's original charcoal and watercolor paintings, we have endeavored to restore the integrity, clarity, and beauty of the artist's work. We too hope these restored editions will play a small part in cultivating the future Mr. Turkle envisioned.

—Rea Berg, Beautiful Feet Books